Merry
Christmas 1996
to Jasmine
from
Mummy & Daddy

This book belongs to

· · · · · · · · · · · · · · · · ·

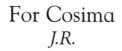

A DORLING KINDERSLEY BOOK

For Cosima
J.R.

For Daisy and Lulu, who
love to dance
S.W.

First published in Great Britain in 1995
by Dorling Kindersley Limited,
9 Henrietta Street, London WC2E 8PS
Reprinted 1996
Text copyright © 1995 Jean Richardson
Illustrations copyright © 1995 Susan Winter

A CIP catalogue record for this book is available
from the British Library.

ISBN 0-7513-7030-4

Colour reproduction by DOT Gradations
Printed and bound in Great Britain by BPC Paulton Books Ltd

THE BEAR WHO WENT TO THE BALLET

JEAN RICHARDSON

Illustrated by SUSAN WINTER

DK

DORLING KINDERSLEY
LONDON • NEW YORK • STUTTGART

Harriet's gran was a genius at giving presents.
They were always very special — and always
what Harriet most wanted.

The present Gran gave her for her seventh birthday was so carefully wrapped that Harriet couldn't guess what was inside. Was it a doll? A book? A game?

Harriet tore off the paper and found – a bear.

But not just any bear. Gran had dressed her as a ballerina. Her frock had a dancer's skirt. A little crown of white flowers perched between her ears. On her feet was a pair of satin ballet shoes just like the ones Harriet wore at her dancing class. Gran had also made her a turquoise tutu and some practice clothes.

The bear was holding an envelope in her paws. On the outside it said: Happy Birthday! Here are tickets for the ballet. Please take me with you!

Harriet was thrilled to find that the tickets were for *The Sleeping Beauty*.

The ballet was wonderful. The bear sat on Harriet's lap and they both clapped and clapped as the ballerina and her prince took lots of curtain calls.

When they got home, before she went to bed, Harriet put the bear with her other toys.

The toys looked at the little bear's ballet frock. They looked at her satin ballet shoes tied with pink ribbon. They looked at her coronet of white flowers.

"Who do you think you are?" asked the oldest doll.

"I'm a ballerina bear," said the little bear shyly.

The toys laughed and laughed. "A ballerina bear! How can a bear be a ballerina? What a silly name for a silly little bear!"

"Ballerinas dance," said the oldest doll, who knew everything. "Let's see you dance."

"I'm too tired," said the bear. And she covered her face with her paws and pretended to fall asleep.

But long after all the other toys had shut their eyes, she was still awake and a very worried little bear. Gran might have dressed her as a ballerina, but she hadn't shown her how to dance.

All the next day the bear worried about how she was going to tell the toys that she couldn't dance. She was afraid they'd all laugh at her even more.

Perhaps the answer was to learn to dance, but how and where? She was still puzzling over this when Harriet came to her rescue.

"Come on, it's time for my dancing class. Let's put on our practice clothes. I don't want to go without you."

It was as though Harriet could read her thoughts.

Ballerina bear watched
the teacher's movements
very carefully.

The class were practising the five positions
that every dancer needs to know. The bear tried
to copy them, but her feet refused to turn out
or cross over.

Then the class moved to the barre,
and practised bending and stretching.
The bear tried stretching her arms,
but her paws were too
short to make a
beautiful circle
above her head.

She liked it best
when everyone
ran round
pretending to be
trees waving in
the breeze. She was
sure she could do that.

That night the toys
started teasing her
again.

"Thinks she's someone
special with her ballet
frock," said one.

"Fancy wearing
flowers in your
hair," said another.

"Let's see you stand on your toes," demanded the elephant rudely.

The little bear felt very sad. She did so want to make friends.

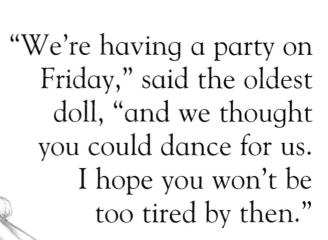

"We're having a party on Friday," said the oldest doll, "and we thought you could dance for us. I hope you won't be too tired by then."

Ballerina bear didn't know what to say.

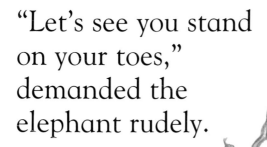

The next day she tried a plié, but her knees wouldn't bend.

She tried to balance on one leg, but she wobbled and wobbled.

She tried to stand on tiptoe . . .

. . . and fell flat on her back.

Finally, she sat on the floor and cried.
"Why am I dressed like a ballerina
if I can't dance?" she sobbed.
She didn't know the answer,
and she felt very sorry for
herself. All she could think
of doing was hiding so
that no one would
find her.

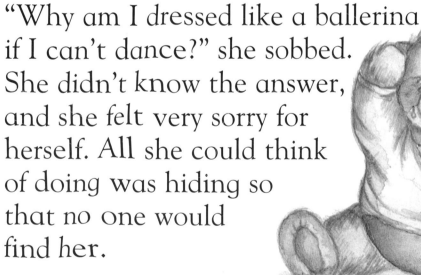

Harriet looked everywhere for her bear.

Under the bed.

In the toy cupboard.

In the bathroom.

Finally, she found her under the settee.

"You silly bear," she said, dusting the bear's fur. "I've been looking for you everywhere. Why are you hiding and looking so sad? Gran's sent us some tickets for the ballet on Saturday."

Harriet doesn't want me to dance, thought the bear, feeling more cheerful. I'm her ballerina bear because I go to the ballet with her. And then she had an idea . . .

The dolls had gone to great trouble for the party. They'd got out the best tea set and found some fizzy lemonade that they called champagne. There were also crisps and some crumbs left over from Harriet's birthday cake.

The bear felt far too nervous to eat anything. She was wearing her turquoise tutu, and the stiff little skirt made her look like a real ballerina. If her great idea didn't work, she thought, she'd have to run away.

Suddenly the oldest doll clapped her hands and everyone stopped talking. "Ladies and gentlemen," she said, "please take your seats. Ballerina bear is going to dance for us."

The toys sat round in a circle. The bear stepped into the middle and curtsied.

"I'm not a dancer," she admitted bravely. "Gran dressed me as a ballerina because Harriet loves dancing and going to the ballet. She took me to see *The Sleeping Beauty*, and I'd like to tell you the story of the ballet."

All the toys
knew the fairy tale,
but the bear made
them see it as a ballet.

When she told
them about the baby
princess's christening, she
described the different dances
of all the fairies who attended,
including the Wicked
Fairy who cast the evil
spell on the princess.

She told them about
the ball to celebrate the
princess's sixteenth birthday,
at which she pricked her
finger and fell asleep. And so
did everyone
else, down to the
smallest page-boy.

She told them how the
princess was woken
up by the kiss of a
handsome prince.

Finally she described the happy ending when the princess's favourite fairy-tale characters danced at her wedding to the prince.

When the bear had finished, at first the toys were very quiet, as if someone had put a magic spell on them. Then they stood up and clapped and cheered as though they were at a real performance.

"Thank you," said the oldest doll, when at last the cheering had died down. "You gave a wonderful performance. You're a real ballerina bear. But it's such a long name for a little bear, so why don't we call you Tutu, after your beautiful ballet skirt?"

The bear nodded. She was too happy to speak.

"And now let's dance," said the oldest doll, so they all chose partners and began to waltz.

When the toys heard that Harriet and Tutu were going to the ballet again, they all crowded to the window to wave as they set off for the theatre.

"We want to know everything that happens," they said, and Tutu promised she'd tell them.

She was wearing her turquoise tutu and a sparkling tiara, and felt very important.

She was sure that she'd be the only ballerina bear at the ballet.